The Hole in Casey's Garden

This book belongs to:

....

Casey, Ben the puppy and Snowy the kitten appear on every
page of this book. Can you find them?

This page is nothing to do with the story, it's just a nice picture to start the book. Many children's books have pages like this. Some people call them the 'endpapers'.

These endpapers were created by Rafa and Alba, aged 4 & 6. They show Casey in a (totally non-scary) rainb dinosaur world. Groar Now read on and enjoy the story...

Written by Gregg Dunnett, Alba Lopez Dunnett (6) & Rafa Lopez Dunnett (4) with help from Casey Waite (7) and Evie Waite (4) - in a campsite, in France, summer 2018.

Inspired by the real hole in Casey's real garden.
Illustrated (beautifully) by Gill Guile.

Endpapers conceived by Alba and Rafa Lopez Dunnett. Rainbow dinosaur, rainbow pterodactyl, all bugs and trees created and coloured by Alba Lopez Dunnett. Rafa Diplodocus and Rafa Monster created and coloured (mostly) by Rafa Lopez Dunnett. Created with help from Maria Lopez (head of scissors) and Gregg Dunnett. Tea drinking by Gregg Dunnett. Clearing up by Maria Lopez.

Cover design and book layout by Cool Water Creative
ISBN: 978-1-912835-04-1

The Hole in Casey's Garden

To Parents, wherever you are...

To learn the story behind this book, please visit
www.greggdunnett.co.uk/caseysgarden

Casey lived in a boring, ordinary house, on a boring, ordinary street, with a totally normal, boring garden.

But one night, he had an **extraordinary** idea.

His little sister was asleep, his father was watching TV, and his mother was in the bath.

Casey sneaked out of bed, crept down the stairs, and squeezed through the cat flap...

He went into the
shed and found
a shovel. Then he
carefully peeled
back the lawn, and
started digging.

He dug all night.

Then he rolled the
lawn back over his
hole, put the shovel
back in the shed,
and went to bed.

The next day, Casey's mum wondered why he was so tired, and why his pyjamas were so muddy.

Casey's dad wondered why there was a small mound of earth at the bottom of the garden.

But they didn't wonder for long.

The next night Casey squeezed
through the cat flap again.
Again he rolled back the lawn.
And again he dug all night.
His hole grew d
          e
           e
            p
             e
              r
               .

The mound of earth at the bottom of the garden grew b i g g e r.

He dug all of Tuesday night, and Wednesday night, and Thursday night and Friday night.

By Saturday night, he had a very big hole indeed.

But no one noticed because he always rolled the lawn back over the top before the sun came up.

His dad thought the mountain of earth at the bottom of the garden must be moles.

The next night Casey built a swimming
pool in his hole. Then he went for a swim.

He swam all night, and there was no one
to tell him to get out when his fingers
went wrinkly.

The next night he built a waterslide that ran from
where Dad kept the lawnmower... All
the
way
to
the box
tom
of the
hole.

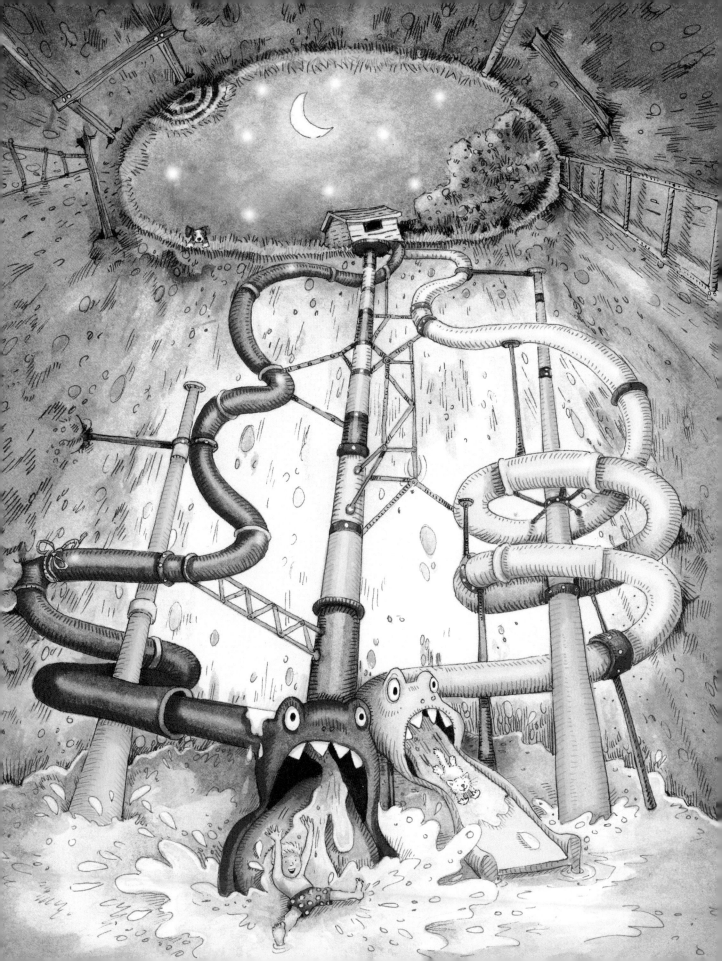

The *next* night he built an adventure playground, with swings, a roundabout, a life-size Tyrannosaurus Rex – with ladders up its back and monkey ropes hanging from its teeth. He built an ice-cream parlour, with free ice-cream, and a bouncy-castle pirate ship.

He was tired again the next day.

The next night Casey invited all his friends from school.

They had *quite* a good party, but there were such a lot of them, the hole wasn't really big enough.

So the next night everyone came back with more shovels, and they made the hole even bigger. They built a racing track, with real red racing cars, a zoo, with penguins, a sailing lake, a cinema with twelve screens, a giant circus tent, and a full size train set with fully working disco-trains.

The next night they had a **super** party.

But the next night, as Casey was creeping down the stairs, he heard a funny noise. A creak, a squeak. And then an enormous **CRASH!**

Then the whole of Casey's house – where his sister was asleep, his father was watching TV and his mother was in the bath – fell into the hole. Then the neighbours' houses fell in, and the school across the road. And the road too.

Everyone was very surprised. At first they all blamed the moles, but soon they found little bits of ice cream parlour, and Casey had to admit that he *might* have had something to do with it.

Casey's daddy was very angry. But he was quite impressed too, since not many children know how to build racing tracks, especially underground.

He told Casey and his friends they had to rebuild the house, the school, the neighbours' houses, the road and the garden. And he helped them do it.

But instead of putting everything back together as it had been before...

Printed in Poland
by Amazon Fulfillment
Poland Sp. z o.o., Wrocław